The
Invisible Seam

Andy William Frew
illustrated by Jun Matsuoka

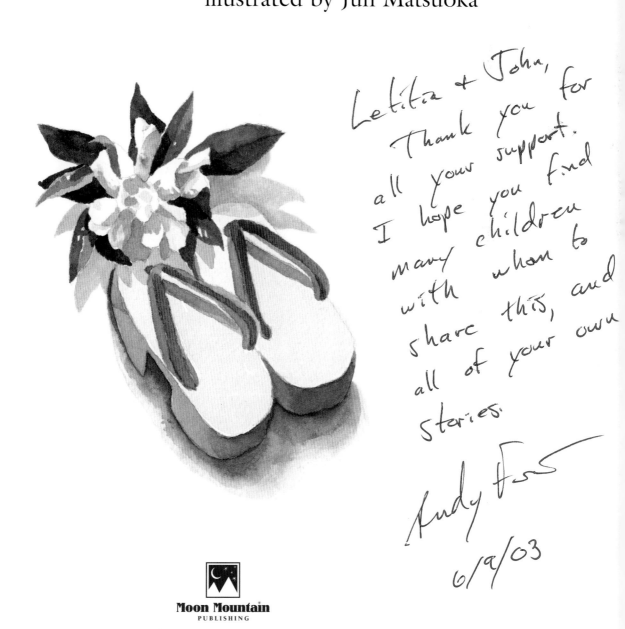

Letitia & John,
Thank you for
all your support.
I hope you find
many children
with whom to
share this, and
all of your own
stories.

Andy Frew
6/9/03

Moon Mountain
PUBLISHING

North Kingstown, Rhode Island

For Cathy, and her mother and great-grandmother
ɷ and ɷ
with special thanks to Kiyoko for sharing her story AWF

To my friend Judi Ito JM

Text Copyright © 2003 Andy William Frew
Illustrations Copyright © 2003 Jun Matsuoka

First edition.

Library of Congress Cataloging-in-Publication Data

Frew, Andrew W., 1944-
  The invisible seam / by Andy William Frew ; illustrated by Jun Matsuoka.
     p. cm.
Summary: A Japanese girl apprenticed to a kimono-maker and entrusted
with an important commission must overcome sabotage from jealous peers
in order to keep a solemn promise that she will always do her best.
  ISBN 1-931659-02-8 (hardcover : alk. paper)
 [1. Sewing—Fiction. 2. Clothing and dress—Fiction. 3.Promises—Fiction.
4. Japan—Fiction.] I. Matsuoka, Jun, ill. II. Title.
  PZ7.F889835 In 2003
  [Fic]—dc21
                              2002011645

Moon Mountain books are available in bulk and with customization for
promotional use. Contact the publisher for details.

Moon Mountain Publishing
80 Peachtree Road
North Kingstown, RI 02852
www.moonmountainpub.com

Jun Matsuoka travelled to Izu, Japan, to sketch many of the restored historic
sites that serve as the settings for *The Invisible Seam*. For the final illustrations,
Jun used watercolors on Arches cold press paper.

Printed in South Korea

10 9 8 7 6 5 4 3 2 1

The
Invisible Seam

Andy William Frew

illustrated by Jun Matsuoka

"Michi, this is Mistress Shinyo. Her family has known ours for many years. You will go with her, and she will see if you are the apprentice she needs."

"But why must I leave you, Aunt Tsuru?"

"I cannot cook for us or do our laundry when my leg is broken."

"I will do it for you."

"No, Michi." Aunt Tsuru gently tapped the wrappings on her leg. "No one can hire me to clean their house, so I cannot buy food. You must go, and I must stay with the doctor. I only hope to get well before we run out of money."

Michi stamped her foot. "I hate the volcano that knocked our house down and broke your leg."

Aunt Tsuru said, "I have taught you better, Michi. Anger will turn your heart bitter. It is no good to hate a mountain. You might as well hate the sky, or the spring weather that blesses us today."

Michi hung her head. "Yes, Aunt Tsuru."

"When I am well, I will come and we will find a new home to replace the one we lost. Till then, you must promise to do your best for Mistress Shinyo."

"Yes, Aunt Tsuru, I promise."

Mistress Shinyo took Michi by the hand. She had stiff, crooked hands, and hardly said a thing on their two day journey.

Mistress Shinyo's house was so large its roof rose high above the tall, wooden fence and blossoming cherry trees. Mistress Shinyo pulled the bell rope by the gate to announce her return.

A broad-shouldered girl came and unlocked the gate. She bowed and said, "It is good to see you home, Mistress Shinyo."

"Michi, this is Taki. She is one of the girls you will be working with."

In the house, their footsteps echoed down long, empty halls that gave Michi a lonely feeling. Taki walked ahead of them into a large room that Mistress Shinyo said was their sewing room.

There were two more girls about Michi's age. One was small and thin; the other was pleasantly chubby. Mistress Shinyo said, "Each girl is working on an *obi* for a different kimono." Taki picked up some deep red material. Mistress Shinyo clucked, "Taki's hands are constantly stained from the garden, and I must give her only dark colors. Over here is Kaoru sewing the lavender cotton, and there, sitting by the flower arrangement, is Hana, sewing the lime-green. You will join them, and I will show you how to work. My house once made the finest ladies' garments in the city, but my crooked hands no longer sew the way they should. Now I am looking for the clever fingers that will give back to this house the reputation it once knew. Listen to me carefully, and I will teach you how to sew every stitch."

Mistress said to Taki, "Show me what you have done."

Taki held up her red *obi* and bowed her head.

Mistress Shinyo looked closely at the work, turned it inside out, then said, "This seam must be done over. It must be tighter. Small and tight. That's how you stitch. Does everyone remember?"

The girls bowed their heads and said, "Yes, Mistress, small and tight."

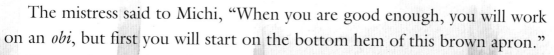

The mistress said to Michi, "When you are good enough, you will work on an *obi*, but first you will start on the bottom hem of this brown apron."

Kaoru, the chubby girl, spoke up. "Mistress, it is nearly noon. Shall I start preparing the mid-day meal?"

Mistress Shinyo nodded, and Kaoru left with an eager smile on her face.

Michi stitched her hem with care. The next day, Mistress Shinyo asked to see Michi's work. "You have done well," said the mistress. "Your stitches are small and tight. The cloth lies smooth and even. I will give you an *obi* today."

When she left, the other girls grumbled. Taki said, "You must think you are very special. It took the rest of us a week to get an *obi*. But if you make us look bad, Mistress will make us work harder. We do not want that."

Michi answered, "I am sorry for any trouble I have caused, but I must keep my promise to my Aunt Tsuru."

Michi kept her promise to her aunt by working hard and learning her skills well. Soon she was working with the most expensive fabrics and the prettiest designs. Mistress gave Taki, Kaoru, and Hana extra practice, hoping they would learn to sew as well as Michi. The three angry girls treated Michi badly. They called her names. They soaked her futon with water. They whispered behind her back. But Mistress gave Michi compliments and rewards for her work. In spite of the girls' mistreatment, Michi was glad to please Mistress Shinyo.

One day the gate bell rang. Taki said to Kaoru, "Our regular customers rattle the gate. Who could be ringing the bell?"

Not long after, Mistress Shinyo entered and said, "An honor has come to our house. The empress has decided her handmaidens will no longer wear plain cotton *obis* to court. Her eldest handmaiden remembers my work and has asked us to make her *obi*. We will make it from this beautiful, gold-colored silk with the wonderful lilies on it. The flowers must be exactly centered on the bow, and the vine is to go exactly around the center of the belt. This is our chance rebuild the House of Shinyo. The *obi* must be perfect."

Michi did not want to cause shame to the other girls, so she said, "This is a job for Taki. I have never worked with such silk. She has been here longest. She should have this honor."

Mistress said, "No, Michi. You will sew the *obi* with the golden lily. Taki works only with dark colors. Besides, she has tried to work with fine silk. She does not have the knack. This must be done with stitches that are so small and so tight that the seams will never be noticed."

Mistress left and Michi sat with the golden lily silk. Taki said, "Be careful how you sew, little girl. Ever since you came to this house, Kaoru's time in the kitchen has been cut in half." Chubby Kaoru scowled. "And Hana barely has time to cut even one flower to brighten the room." Little Hana's nose wrinkled angrily. "And I have not seen the garden for days. If you do too well, and we lose any more time for doing what we really want, you will regret it."

Michi felt sorry for the girls, but she had to keep her promise to her aunt. Long after the other girls had gone to bed, Michi sat and worked by lantern light.

In the morning, Mistress Shinyo came to the sewing room and asked to see Michi's work on the *obi* with the golden lily. She gave it to her, and Mistress said, "Michi, you have finished. I did not expect this so soon. And the stitching is so small and so tight, even when I look closely at the seam, I cannot see the thread." To the other girls she said, "Do you see what can be done if you learn your skills well? You will spend an extra hour after supper practicing your stitches, small and tight."

Mistress left to inform the empress' handmaiden. Taki said, "You will pay for this. You won't know when it will come, but we will make you pay."

Michi was afraid. She turned to face the corner, thinking about her promise to her aunt. If only there was some way to be free of it. But no—it was more than the promise. Aunt Tsuru had taught her that she must always respect her elders, do her work well, and do what is right no matter what. There had been no other way.

Michi didn't sleep well. Dawn came and still she worried what the girls might do. She rose and rubbed her eyes. As she left her room, Mistress Shinyo rushed into the hallway. Michi had never seen her so excited. "Michi…" She was out of breath. She glanced at Taki, Kaoru, and Hana, but spoke to Michi. "…an even greater honor has come. A powerful lord from Osaka has arrived. He and his beautiful wife will be presented at the emperor's court in a few days. The empress' handmaiden told her about us. We are to make the kimono she will wear. She will be here today."

Taki, Kaoru, and Hana traded excited glances. Could it be true that the House of Mistress Shinyo would once again make kimonos for ladies who were to be presented at court? Mistress Shinyo said, "Michi, you will make the kimono. The seams must be perfect. The silk will be the purest white with orchids all through it. Come. The fitting room must be made ready." Michi followed. Taki, Kaoru, and Hana watched her leave. In their eyes, Michi saw jealous anger.

That afternoon, the bell rang. The beautiful lady from Osaka and her servant swept gracefully into the fitting room. As Michi helped Mistress Shinyo measure the beautiful lady, Michi noticed how she wore her kimono snug in the middle. The beautiful lady's servant watched with a sharp eye as they measured. When they were done, the servant nodded to her lady, then said to Mistress Shinyo, "You will receive the silk tomorrow."

The white silk with orchids arrived an hour before lunch. "At last," said Mistress Shinyo. Michi washed her hands so they would be clean as she worked with the white silk. Carefully, she carried the cloth to her seat in the sewing room.

Michi started with the bottom hem. Mistress said, "Good, Michi. If there was a chance of a mistake, the bottom hem was the place to make it. But your stitches are small and tight. Next comes the inside of the *sode*. You must remember, the lady's arms must fit comfortably. Go eat your lunch now. Hunger must not keep you from thinking about your stitches."

After lunch, Michi stitched the *sode*. Mistress checked and said, "Well done, Michi. You have the feel of the cloth. Your stitches are small and tight. Now do the outside seam."

Michi sewed the outside of the *sode*. Mistress checked it and said, "Well done, Michi. Your stitches are small and tight. Next do the *migoro*. The sides and the back must hang straight and even. It will take even more care. But you have worked hard all afternoon. Eat your supper before you go on."

After supper, Michi found Taki, Kaoru, and Hana carrying their sewing cases out of the sewing room. Taki said, "You will work best with quiet. We asked Mistress if we can practice in our sleeping quarters. We do not want to bother you."

Michi bowed her head, saying, "Thank you for the kind thought," and sat down to her work. She took the smallest needle from her sewing case and opened her box of thread. To her horror, she saw that all the thread in her box was red.

Michi instantly knew what the girls had done. Tears flowed from her eyes. How could she use such a color with pure white silk? Even one strand of red showing through would ruin the kimono. As she squeezed her eyes shut to stop the tears, a vision of Aunt Tsuru floated before her. Michi's aunt said, "You made a promise. Now do the right thing."

Michi opened her eyes and looked at the red thread. She had sewed the golden lily *obi* with stitches that were so small and tight, Mistress could not see the thread. This time even the seams would be invisible.

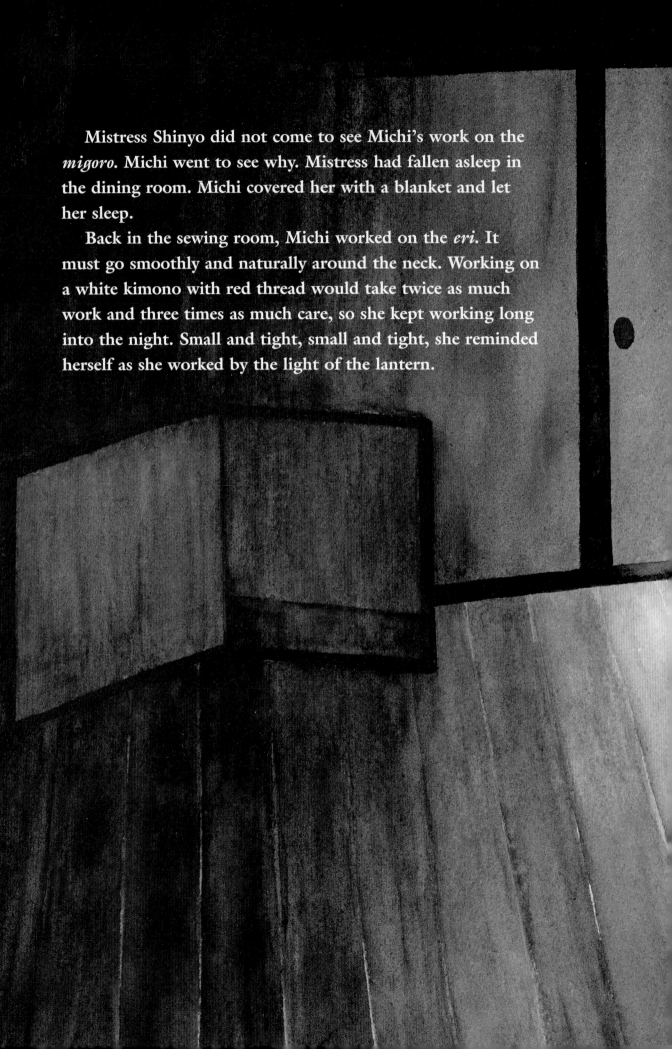

Mistress Shinyo did not come to see Michi's work on the *migoro*. Michi went to see why. Mistress had fallen asleep in the dining room. Michi covered her with a blanket and let her sleep.

Back in the sewing room, Michi worked on the *eri*. It must go smoothly and naturally around the neck. Working on a white kimono with red thread would take twice as much work and three times as much care, so she kept working long into the night. Small and tight, small and tight, she reminded herself as she worked by the light of the lantern.

It was mid-morning before Mistress Shinyo rose and went to the sewing room. Michi had fallen asleep after tying the last stitch. The mistress picked up the kimono with a smile, but when she turned it inside out and saw the stitches, her smile disappeared. "Red!" she shouted. Michi awoke. "Michi, how could you? This kimono must be perfect, and you have sewn white silk with red thread. I will be ruined."

Michi bowed her head and said nothing.

The gate bell rang, and the beautiful lady with the sharp-eyed servant glided into the fitting room. "Mistress Shinyo," said the servant, dignified and elegant, "we hope we have not caused a problem by arriving early. The lady wishes to see your progress. Bring the kimono."

Taki, Kaoru, and Hana were giggling behind a curtain. After this, Michi might never sew again. They could go back to working the way they had before.

Mistress Shinyo could not disobey such an important lady. She tried to hide the red stitches. The beautiful lady was happy to see it finished. The servant patiently wrapped it around the lady, stopping here for a tuck, there to smooth it. The fit was perfect. The beautiful lady smiled. The sharp-eyed servant bowed to the lady, then said to Mistress Shinyo, "How clever, Mistress Shinyo. Inside, the red thread challenges me to find a flaw in the stitching. Outside, even the seams are invisible. This is a kimono worthy of the emperor's court." She paid Mistress Shinyo generously. The beautiful lady put her hand on her servant's arm and whispered in her ear. The servant nodded, smiled, and said, "We will be having our stitching done here from now on."

Mistress bowed farewell, then went to the sewing room. Michi was in the corner, her head silently bowed. She couldn't tell if the mistress was angry or relieved. The tears in Mistress Shinyo's eyes finally fell, and she asked, "Michi, how could you take such a risk? We could have lost our only chance for a decent living."

Michi kneeled before Mistress Shinyo and said, "I am deeply ashamed. I have treated my teacher badly. She should punish me."

Mistress Shinyo raised her hand.

"Mistress," Taki stepped from behind the curtain with her head down. Kaoru and Hana followed.

The mistress turned to Taki and asked, "What do you want?"

"I must confess. Michi had to use red thread because I took all her other colors. She had no choice if she was to do the work."

Mistress asked, "Michi, why didn't you tell me this?"

"I do the work that has been given to me, and I do the best I can."

Mistress Shinyo looked sternly at the girls. "Taki, Kaoru, and Hana, you will stay in your sleeping quarters, where you will do your sewing from sun-up to sun-down till I can forgive you. You will work and think about what you almost did to this household. If Michi had not been so skillful, we might never have recovered. Who would care for your precious garden then, Taki?"

Michi spoke up, "Mistress, please don't punish them. They were unhappy because they do not have the same gift as me. If your good name was based on something else, they would be in my place and I would be in theirs. Taki is a far better gardener than I; Kaoru prepares our meals much better than I ever could; and Hana has a touch with flower arrangements that seems magic."

☙   ❧

Aunt Tsuru thanked the doctor. "My leg is healed because of your kindness and skill."

"You still walk with a limp. Stay with me for another week," said the doctor.

"I have no more money, and my family has always paid its way. Thank you, but no. It is time for me to go and join my niece."

Because of her limp, it took Aunt Tsuru three days of traveling in summer heat before reaching the house of Mistress Shinyo. She rang the bell, and a smiling girl with dirty hands opened the gate. The girl bowed, then went back to working in the beautiful garden around the house. Michi's face appeared at the window. She gave a happy squeal and ran down the path to give her aunt a hug.

Mistress Shinyo waited at the door to greet her. "Welcome to our house." Aunt Tsuru removed her sandals and entered. Near the door, an elegant arrangement of red and white roses scented the air.

Aunt Tsuru said, "What a beautiful house you have, Mistress Shinyo."

"It has not always been so," said the mistress. "But come and rest. You must be tired after your long journey. Will you have something to eat?"

Wonderful smells came from the kitchen, and Aunt Tsuru said, "You are kind to an old woman. What can I ever do in return?"

Mistress Shinyo said, "You and your niece can stay with us in this old house, so that it may once again become what it was."

Names and Terms

Michi = roadway
Tsuru = crane
Shinyo = needle
Taki = waterfall
Kaoru = aroma
Hana = flower

eri: collar
migoro: body of the garment
obi: broad sash tied at the waist of a kimono
sode: sleeve

For lesson plans and related resources, visit www.moonmountainpub.com